To Daniele and Drew

E
FRA

Published by Roaring Brook Press
Roaring Brook Press is a division of Holtzbrinck Publishing Holdings Limited Partnership
175 Fifth Avenue, New York, New York 10010
www.roaringbrookpress.com

Distributed in Canada by H. B. Fenn and Company Ltd.

Library of Congress Cataloging-in-Publication Data
Frazier, Craig, 1955-
Hank finds inspiration / Craig Frazier.—1st ed.
p. cm.
Summary: Hank the snake and his human friend, Stanley, each go to the city in search of
inspiration, but Hank's journey is a failure until he returns home.
ISBN-13: 978-1-59643-358-8
ISBN-10: 1-59643-358-2
[1. Inspiration—Fiction. 2. Snakes—Fiction. 3. Human-animal relationships—Fiction.] I. Title.
PZ7.F869Han 2008
[E]—dc22
2007047919

Roaring Brook Press books are available for special promotions and premiums.
For details contact: Director of Special Markets, Holtzbrinck Publishers.

First Edition September 2008
Printed in China

10 9 8 7 6 5 4 3 2 1

Hank
FINDS INSPIRATION

Craig Frazier

A NEAL PORTER BOOK
ROARING BROOK PRESS
NEW YORK

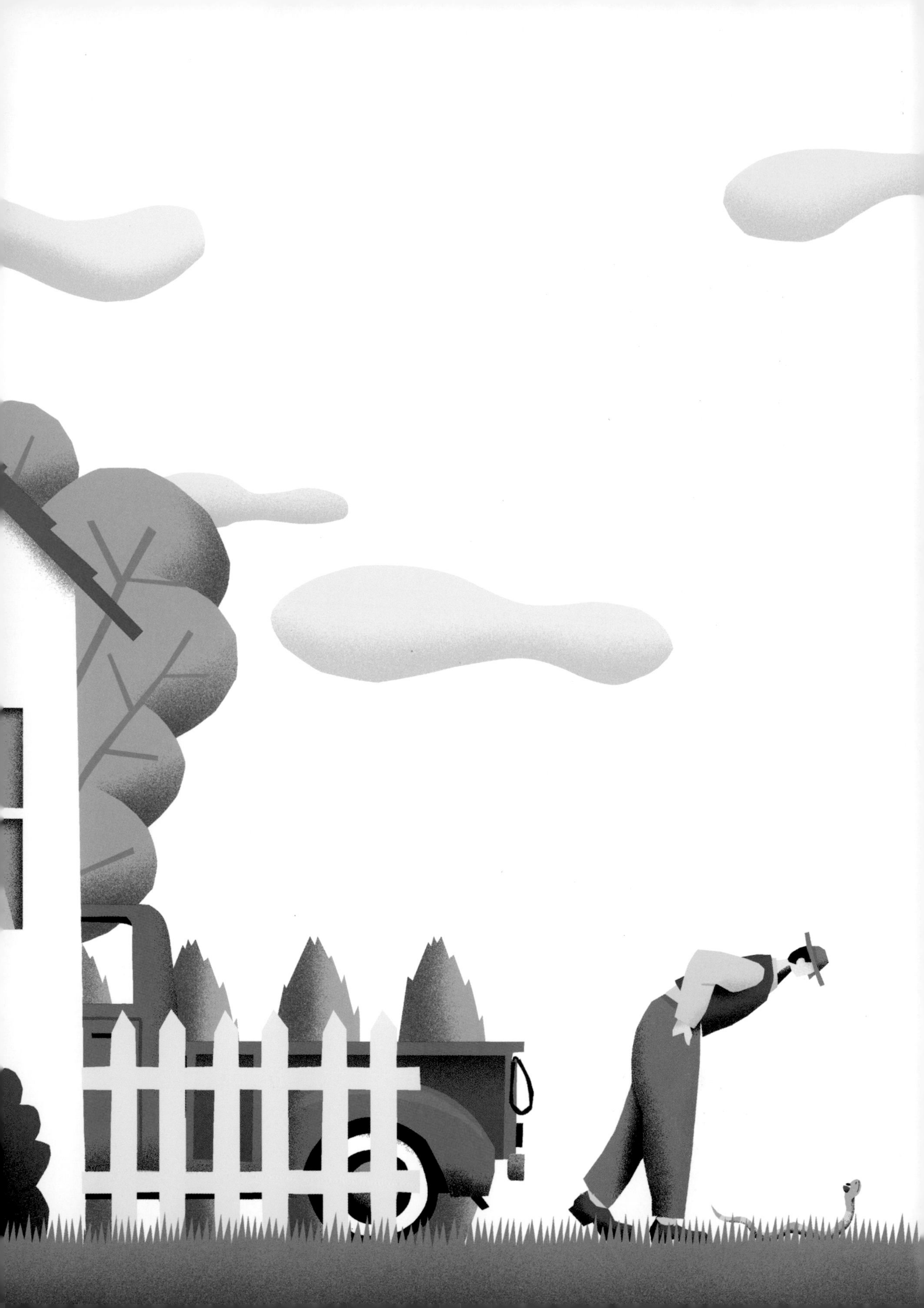

"I wish our yard wasn't so flat and boring," sighed Stanley.

"I wish I could touch the clouds," said his friend Hank the snake.

"We need some inspiration, Hank. That'll fix things," said Stanley.

"See you later, Hank. I'm off to the city to look for inspiration," said Stanley as he sped off.

"Hey, I need some, too!" yelled Hank.

Hank jumped in a cab. "To the city please.
I'm going to find some inspiration!"

Hank got out at 51st and Burnham. "Whoa, this city is big! I have no idea where to find inspiration."

"Pardon me, I'm told that I can get inspiration here."

"Hmmm," said the man, who seemed kind of grumpy. "This is where I get the day's news. You might try the library a block uptown."

"Thank you, and sorry to disturb you," said Hank.

"Excuse me, ma'am. Can I find inspiration here?" Hank whispered.

"It depends on what you are interested in. I think you might find it at Dunphy Park," said the lady, smiling sweetly.

"Hi. I don't mean to interrupt you, but I understand I can find inspiration here."

"This is a lovely place to enjoy nature, but I always find inspiration listening to the jazz trio at the end of the park," said the nice man.